A. Beasty Bites
B. Jungle Java
C. Savanna Library
D. House of Bones
E. Amazon Security
F. Everyday School
G. Wild'n'Wooly
   Barber Shop
H. Arctic House
   Post Office
I. Monkey Bowl
J. Porpoise Pool
K. Big Cat Toys
L. Gator Grocery

Hayley

Harley

Pouch

Baa-a-a-b

Midge & Pidge

Boyd

Dedicated to all children everywhere who love to read.

—J. M.

To Andrew and Jenni

—M.S.

ZONDERKIDZ

The Perfect Christmas Pageant
Copyright © 2013 by Joyce Meyer
Illustrations © 2013 by Zondervan

Requests for information should be addressed to:

Zonderkidz, 5300 Patterson Ave SE, Grand Rapids, Michigan 49530

ISBN: 978-0-310-72354-7

Joyce Meyer is represented by Thomas J. Winters of Winters, King & Associates, Inc., Tulsa, Oklahoma.

Zonderkidz is a trademark of Zondervan.

Illustrator: Mary Sullivan
Contributors: Jill Gorey, Nancy Haller
Editor: Barbara Herndon
Art direction and design: Cindy Davis

Printed in China

13 14 15 /LPC/ 10 9 8 7 6 5 4 3 2 1

EVERYDAY ZOO

JOYCE MEYER

The Perfect Christmas Pageant

pictures by MARY SULLIVAN

ZONDERkidz

It was the Christmas season at Everyday Zoo, and the whole town glistened, glittered, and glowed.

But nothing sparkled as brightly as Hayley Hippo's spirits, because she had been chosen to direct this year's Christmas pageant.

Last year the Bunny family had been in charge of the production—all 25 of them!
Babs Bunny's performance as Mary was amazing. And what a sweet baby Jesus!

The music, the costumes, the manger made of carrots . . . EVERYTHING was wonderful.

Hayley was determined to make this year's pageant the best one yet. When she arrived at the theater, Pouch smiled as he handed her copies of the script. "I'm sure you know what the Christmas story is about," he said.

Hayley nodded. "Oh, yes! It's all about the birth of Christ!"

Hayley's eyes sparkled as she imagined how spectacular the play would be. It would be her special Christmas gift to Jesus. And it would be perfect.

The first thing Hayley needed was a great cast.
She searched high and low for the perfect baby Jesus ...

"Um, not quite ...
right for the role."

Then she ran into Miss Bimble and her adorable nephew, Baa-a-a-b.

"Oh, Miss Bimble! Baa-a-a-b is so cute and cuddly! Do you think he could play baby Jesus in the Christmas pageant?"

"That's a splendid idea, dear!"

After Hayley cast the rest of the roles, it was time for rehearsals to begin. Unfortunately, things didn't go as smoothly as she expected.

The angel Gabriel was too LOUD ...

The innkeeper was downright dangerous …

The shepherds kept losing their way …

Joseph couldn't remember his lines …

And Baa-a-a-b got his hair cut!

Hayley was disappointed. She wanted the pageant to be perfect.
So she worked hard to try and fix the problems.

When it was time to start building the sets, everyone worked hard to make them the best they could be.

Rehearsals were finally going well, until Boyd ran in carrying one of the angels.
"Baa-a-a-b ate off the wings! What are we going to do?"
"I had a feeling he was teething," Miss Bimble said sheepishly.

"This won't do," Hayley announced. "We shouldn't have cardboard angels anyway. This play is about the birth of Jesus! We need something spectacular!" That's when Hayley had her best idea yet.

"You want *us* to be angels?" asked Midge.
"But we're flightless birds, gumdrop!" said Pidge.
"You'll be suspended by ropes and pulleys," Hayley said.
"Ropes and pulleys?!" cried Midge.

"I suppose that could work …"

"You'll make the best angels ever," Hayley assured them.

"Well ... okay. Sign us up!" said Pidge.

Hayley gave her friends a big hug. "I promise it will be perfect!"

With Midge and Pidge set to make their flying debut, it was time for the final rehearsal. Harley was so excited he forgot one of his lines …

"We will sleep on your table."

This made Boyd and Arnold start to giggle.

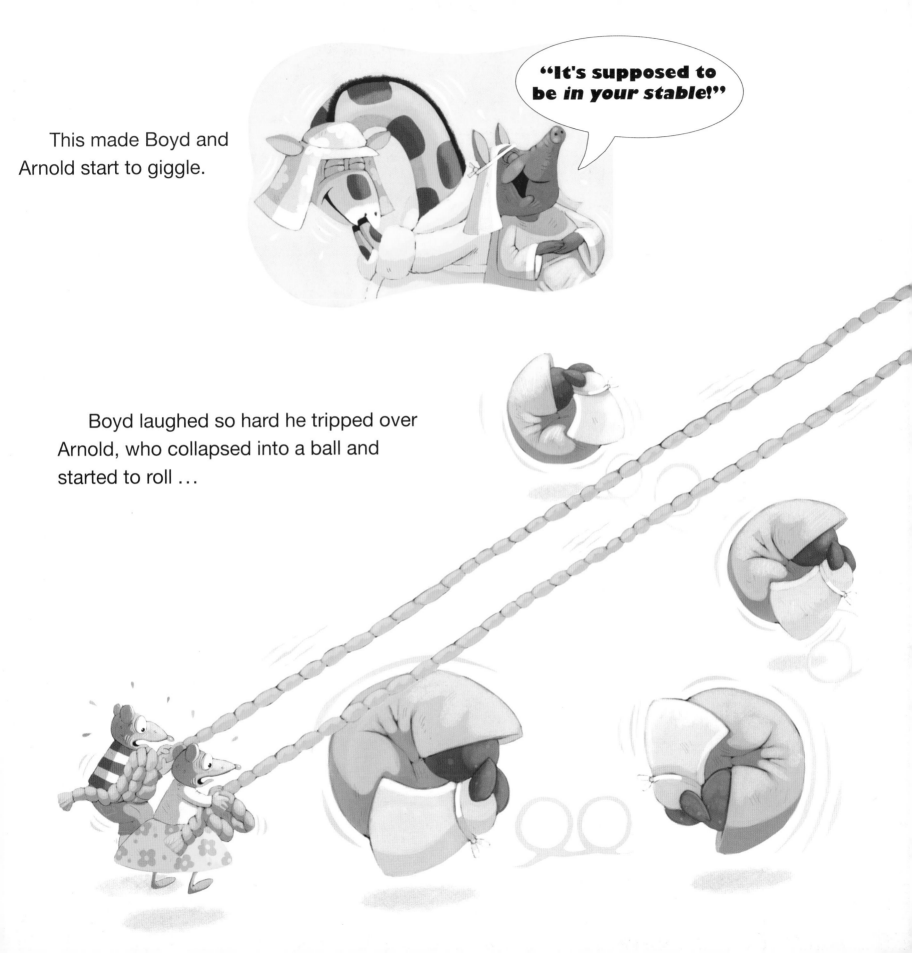

"It's supposed to be *in your stable!*"

Boyd laughed so hard he tripped over Arnold, who collapsed into a ball and started to roll …

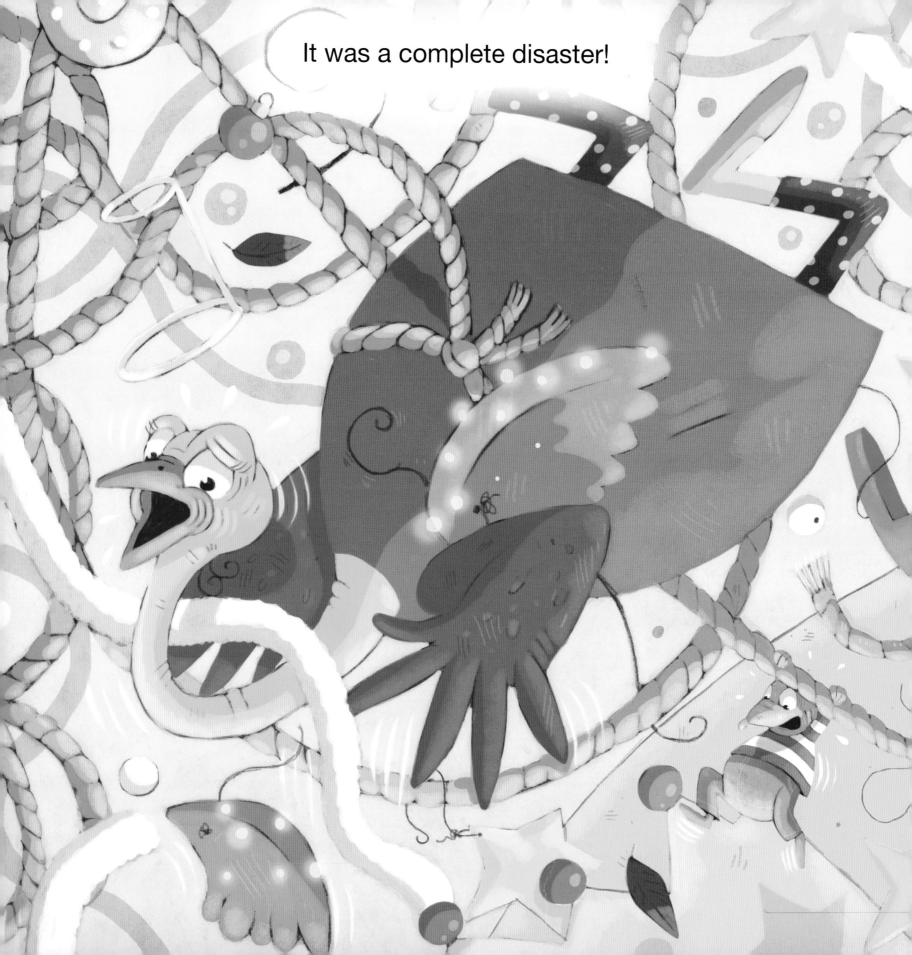

It was a complete disaster!

A tear rolled down Hayley's cheek as she looked at the mess around her. "The pageant is ruined!"

Harley gave her a hug. "Don't cry, Hayley."

"But I wanted everything to be perfect!" she sniffled.

"I'm sure that's what Mary and Joseph wanted too, that first Christmas," Pouch said. "But things weren't perfect for them either."

"Goodness, no!" said Midge. "They were exhausted from their long trip."

"Poor Mary was about to have a baby," clucked Pidge. "And they had to sleep in a stable!"

"But do you know the one thing that was perfect that night?" Pouch asked.

Hayley thought for a moment, and then her eyes grew wide. "Jesus," she said, finally understanding. "*He* was perfect. That's what the Christmas story is all about!"

Hayley quietly picked up a hammer and some broken wood and headed for the door.

"Where are you going?" Harley asked.

"To build a stable," Hayley replied.

"Wait!" Boyd shouted. "You forgot the lights!"

"I don't think we'll be needing those," she said.

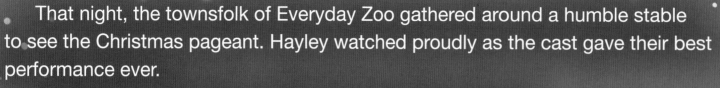

That night, the townsfolk of Everyday Zoo gathered around a humble stable to see the Christmas pageant. Hayley watched proudly as the cast gave their best performance ever.

"Unto you this day is born a Savior!" an angel announced.

"Wrapped in swaddling cloths and lying in a manger," declared another.

"We will go to Bethlehem to see him!" the shepherds shouted exuberantly.

Suddenly, one star, brighter than the rest, seemed to shine down, lighting up Mary, Joseph, and their baby.

Mary smiled at her visitors. "His name is Jesus," she said proudly.

"He's Christ the Lord!" Joseph beamed. "Isn't he awesome?"

Under a starry night sky, a group of friends celebrated the birth of our Savior, Jesus Christ, just like the holy family and the shepherds did so many years ago.

Everyone, including the Bunny family, thought the celebration was wonderful.

It wasn't perfect ... but somehow it was just right.